# Sky Dancer

*For Jenny, my sky dancer.*

— JB

The illustrations in this book were done in watercolor paints. The display type was set in Fine Hand. The text was set in Windsor.
Printed and bound by Tien Wah Press. Production supervision by Esilda Kerr. Designed by Charlotte Hommey.

Inquiries should be addressed to Lothrop, Lee & Shepard Books, a division of William Morrow & Company, Inc.,
1350 Avenue of the Americas, New York, New York 10019.
Printed in Singapore
First Edition    1 2 3 4 5 6 7 8 9 10
Library of Congress Cataloging in Publication Data
Bushnell, Jack. Sky Dancer / by Jack Bushnell; illustrated by Jan Ormerod.
p.  cm.  Summary: One winter morning Jenny discovers a hawk has come to the farm,
and she develops a rapport with the graceful sky dancer.
ISBN 0-688-05288-6. — ISBN 0-688-05289-4 (lib.bdg.)  [1. Hawks—Fiction. 2. Freedom—Fiction. 3. Farm life—Fiction.]
I. Ormerod, Jan, ill. II. Title. PZ7.B96547Sk 1996 [E]—dc20  94-24577

# SKY DANCER

Jack Bushnell

Jan Ormerod

LOTHROP, LEE & SHEPARD BOOKS • NEW YORK

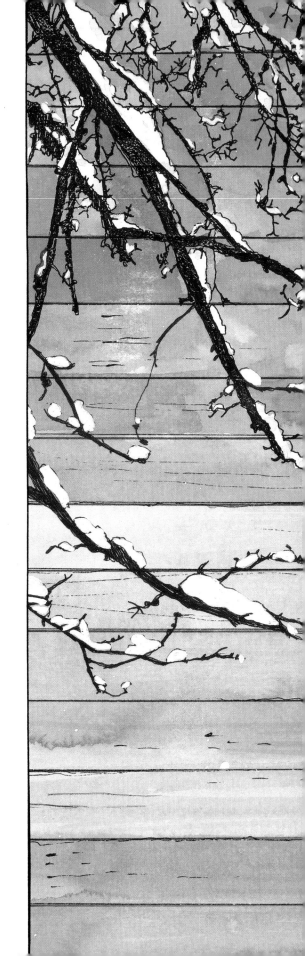

W HEN THE FEBRUARY SUN ROSE BEHIND
her house that morning, Jenny was already awake, wrapped
in a blanket at the foot of her bed, looking through the
icy window.

A new snow covered the backyard. Beyond the fence, the
pumpkin field lay white and still. In the distance, skeletons of
trees stood, black against the winter sunrise.

JENNY GOT OUT OF BED AND DRESSED QUIETLY, THEN TIPTOED downstairs so she wouldn't wake her father. She put on her boots and jacket, wrapped a scarf around her neck and mouth, pulled on her mittens, and opened the back door.

The icy air bit her cheeks and brought tears to her eyes as she walked across the yard, making the first footprints of the day in the fresh snow. Soon it would be time to collect eggs from the henhouse, time to feed the pigs in the barn. But for now the morning was hers.

She opened a gate and walked into the pumpkin field. No breeze blew. No birds sang.

SUDDENLY A HIGH SHRIEK EXPLODED IN THE AIR.
"Keeeeeeeeer!"

Jenny jumped and screamed. A huge bird, a hawk, swooped
in front of her, one wing almost touching the ground,
the other pointing toward the sky. The streaked white of
the hawk's chest and the separate feathers, like fingers,
at the tips of its broad wings stood out clearly. Wing tip
to wing tip, it was taller than she was.

It left as suddenly as it had come. Flashing rusty red tail feathers and crying out again, it soared across the field. Jenny stood staring, wishing she could follow it through the air.

"What happened?" her father yelled, hurrying toward her from the house. His breath billowed about his face.

Jenny was surprised to see him there. She had forgotten her scream. "A hawk, Dad," she said as he came up beside her. "I'm okay. Did you see it?"

Her father gazed over her head. Jenny looked in the same direction. Across the white field, high in the bare branches of a tall oak tree, sat the bird.

FOR THE REST OF THE DAY, THE HAWK SAT ON THAT BRANCH.
It didn't fly closer or circle overhead. And it didn't fly away.
Wherever she was, collecting eggs or making snow angels
beside the barn, Jenny could have sworn that it was
watching her.

The next morning, Jenny couldn't wait to get outside.
Just before she saw the hawk, she heard a rustling in the
air. Above her, the bird spread its wings across the sky. It
hovered, watching her, its head cocked to one side. Then it
tilted its body and, with a flash of red, flew up to its branch
in the oak tree.

Jenny pretended to explore the pumpkin field, hoping not to frighten the hawk. "Is it my red hair?" she whispered. "Do you think I'm a hawk, too?"

The air rustled. Jenny looked up. The hawk had moved to a closer tree. It watched her calmly.

"Are you following me?" she asked, her heart pounding. "Are you looking for a friend?" The hawk hunched its shoulders.

Her father had to call her three times before she went in to breakfast.

LATER THAT MORNING, JENNY AND HER DAD DROVE INTO TOWN.
They bought chicken feed, groceries, and two new snow tires,
then went to Loretta's Diner for lunch.

Loretta's was full of farmers, their sleeves rolled up in the
warm, stuffy air, their boots dripping melted snow onto
Loretta's clean floor. At one of the tables, Ben Parker was
talking angrily.

"I first noticed it a week ago," he said. "Scattered snow.
A couple of feathers. Sure enough, one of my hens was
missing."

"I've lost one myself," said Jenny's father.

"Sounds like a hawk," said Billy Pacheko. "A hawk's wings
will mess up the snow pretty good."

"That's what I figured," said Ben. "I've lost three of my
best egg-layers already, and I can't afford to lose any more."

"As far as I'm concerned," said Owen Tibbs, "you can take
all the hawks and coyotes you can find and drop 'em off the
edge of the earth. I wouldn't miss 'em."

JENNY SHIVERED. SHE THOUGHT OF ALL THE TIMES SHE HAD watched hawks circling high above her, turning and turning in slow, graceful spirals. She had her own special name for them: sky dancers. When she was little, she had wanted to be a sky dancer, too.

"I know it's against the law," Ben said, "but I might go hawk hunting one of these days." The other men said nothing. They understood how Ben felt.

As Jenny and her father left Loretta's and climbed into their truck, Dad said, "I have an idea I know where Ben's hawk is." Jenny said nothing.

THE NEXT MORNING, JENNY SAT AT THE FOOT OF HER BED, wrapped in a blanket. The sun had risen less than an hour ago, but already the bird was there. It was there the next morning, too, and the next, but she did not go to it. Still, she felt its eyes, searching the field, the yard, the windows of the house.

By the afternoon of the third day, Jenny could resist the bird no longer. As she walked toward the tree, the hawk sat hunched and still.

"Why are you here?" she asked. "You shouldn't stay. They'll come after you." She picked up a stone and threw it at the hawk to scare it off, but she wasn't strong enough to reach it.

Jenny stood there in the snow until her toes grew cold. When the sun set and the hawk turned deep black, like a hole in the sky above her, she walked back to the house.

"BEN PARKER LOST ANOTHER CHICKEN," DAD TOLD HER at breakfast the next day. Jenny stared at her bowl. "I told him the hawk out back might be the one."

Jenny swallowed hard. "It's not the one," she told him. "It's not here for chickens. It's here for . . ."

Dad leaned forward. "Here for what, sweetheart?"

HERE FOR ME, she wanted to say, but she wasn't even sure what that meant. So she just shook her head. "I don't know. Here for something else."

Her father shrugged. "Well, we've got work to do."

ALL THROUGH HER CHORES, JENNY THOUGHT ABOUT THE hawk. It had never been penned in like her dad's hens or pigs. It went wherever it liked. And it had chosen to come here. To her.

When Jenny walked out of the barn, a man was standing in the pumpkin field. He wore a long, heavy coat and a hat with earflaps. He carried a rifle.

Jenny ducked behind the henhouse fence. Through the chicken wire, she watched the man walk carefully in the snow. It was Ben Parker. He was looking at the hawk.

When he stopped, Jenny held her breath. He lifted the rifle. Jenny felt sick to her stomach. Clenching her fists, she ran from behind the fence. "Daddeeeeeee!" she shrieked. Ben turned toward her, lowering his gun. Dad hurried out of the barn.

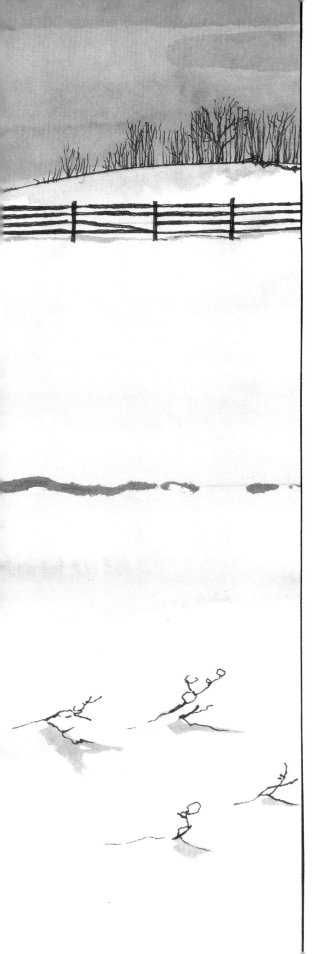

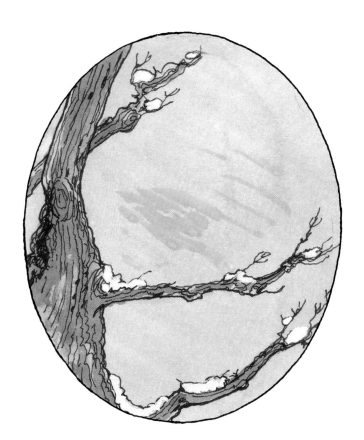

"WHAT'S THE TROUBLE?" BEN ASKED. HIS VOICE CUT HARSHLY through the crisp air.

Jenny's father wiped his hands with a rag. "My girl doesn't think this is your hawk," he said.

"Is that right?" said Ben. Jenny heard the anger in his voice. "What does SHE know?"

Jenny's face felt hot and her voice sounded loud as she answered, "I know it sits here every day and never moves. Whenever I look, it's there." She took a deep breath. "It's not the one."

"What if it IS?" Ben asked, looking at Jenny's father.

Dad laid his hand on Jenny's shoulder. "If it is," he said, "we'll make it up to you, Ben."

All three of them looked back to where the hawk had been, but it was gone.

THAT AFTERNOON, WHILE DAD READ IN FRONT OF THE FIRE, Jenny couldn't sit still. She prowled the house. She looked out the kitchen window, then the living room window. She climbed the stairs and looked out her bedroom window. But the hawk wasn't there. What if Ben had scared it away for good? What if she never found out for certain why it had come?

At bedtime, the phone rang. "Ben shot a hawk going after one of his hens," Dad told her when he hung up. "It wasn't a redtail."

NEXT MORNING IT FELT WARMER THAN IT HAD FOR MONTHS. Icicles dripped under the eaves. A few blades of pale green grass poked up through the melting snow.

Jenny crossed the yard to the pumpkin field and opened the gate. The hawk sat in its tree, dark and silent, staring back at her.

Suddenly it crouched and raised its wings. Then it leapt forward and flew out of the shadows and into the early morning light. Its head thrust forward, its eyes glinting in the sun, it flew straight toward Jenny. Jenny's legs went weak and her heart pounded in her ears.

The hawk seemed to grow, its wings spreading across the field. Just as it reached Jenny, it rose and passed overhead. But it now flew in a way she'd never seen before. Dipping and rising, it seemed to follow the outlines of invisible hills. Down into an unseen valley it fell, its wings tucked against its body. Then up to the summit, wings outspread.

IT CIRCLED THE FIELD LIKE THAT, THEN HEADED BACK TOWARD
her. Rises followed dips, like waves gliding toward a beach.
Jenny laughed and lifted her arms as if she, too, would fly.
She felt the dance of the hawk in her own body, and she ran
toward it through the snow. Panting, running, laughing, she
chased the hawk along the ground as it swooped and soared
above her. Her boots sent up sprays of snow. Her hair came
loose from her scarf and streamed behind her.

WHEN SHE COULD RUN NO LONGER, JENNY STOPPED
to catch her breath. A gentle breeze brushed her face.

"So long, sky dancer," she yelled as the hawk flew toward
the far end of the field. Gradually it rose, its wings beating
slowly. For several seconds, it seemed to hang motionless,
suspended in the air. She wished it would stay there forever.

Then, as Jenny watched, the hawk cleared the treetops
and disappeared into the warm light of an early spring.